Picture it & Write
Volume 1

Fiction and poetry inspired by photographs.

By Ermilia and contributors

ISBN: 0984930884
ISBN-13: 978-0-9849308-8-3

ACKNOWLEDGMENTS

Ermisenda and Eliabeth would like to thank all of the Picture it & Write contributors who made this publication possible. Thank you for turning our weekly writing prompt into a community. Many of you are regulars and have a special place in our hearts. We hope that this publication can be a token of our gratitude and highlight the good that can come from collaboration. May we all continue to write wherever our paths lead us. Special thanks to Kris Atkinson for taking the time to edit the submissions.

A comprehensive list of contributors with a link to their blogs is at the end of the book.

We hope the community continues to grow, so please invite others to join the fun at ermiliablog.wordpress.com.

All profits from the sale of this publication go to The Girl Effect, a movement to change the world one girl at a time. Learn more about this cause at girleffect.org.

CONTENTS

The Stuff of Legends
By Anne Schilde

Angie tottered across the map on her silver pointe shoes. Long elegant legs of silver stretched from her tiny silver tutu. She stopped and stood peering contemptuously down at Gordy where he lay. Gordy's golden trousers were dropped, unabashedly revealing his intricate anatomy for all to see. What his nakedness revealed, however mysterious, appeared useless in the sense of things.

Cartography was a dance for only a skilled dancer. Gordy was clearly no dancer. Exposing himself that way, he wasn't apt to be a person of any kind of elegance.

"What kind of dancer are you?" Angie scoffed.

"I'm no dancer," Gordy replied, fanning his parts immodestly. "I am a compass!"

Angie gasped. "A compass? Why, you don't look anything like a compass! You don't have elegant legs that dance on needles. You are round and fat and you haven't a needle about you!"

"My needle is right there before your eyes," Gordy retorted. "You are just ashamed to see it in all its beauty."

"What use is a needle like that for cartography?" Angie asked. She danced across the map and back again. "My pirouette defines a range. My deboulé can measure the distances between points and bisect lines or arcs. Can you bisect a line with that needle of yours?"

"Well, no," admitted Gordy.

"What kind of compass are you then, if you can't bisect

a line?" Angie snitted.

"Well, what kind of compass are you if you can't find North?" Gordy snitted back.

Angie was mad. North was plainly drawn on the map. It was plainly drawn on every map she'd ever danced. "I don't have to find North, it's already been found!" she snapped.

"And who do you think found it?"

"Not you," Angie said mimicking Gordy's voice.

"Yes me," he mimicked back. "That is my needle you see there on that map."

"Ew! You're disgusting!" Angie cried. "Is it not enough that you wave it about in the open like that?"

"You are just jealous in that little pin head of yours," Gordy offered proudly. "My needle is on that map because it's legendary. Every cartographer and every navigator has gazed fondly upon my needle. Why, I even saw you look fondly upon it as well when you danced up."

"I did no such thing!"

"Denying it will do you no good."

"You're impossible!" Angie bristled.

Gordy was as crass in his mind as he was in his manner. How could he call himself a compass in either case? And she did not look upon it fondly. She distinctly remembered it was contemptuously. She could never be fond of a needle like that.

"If I'm a compass and you're a compass," Gordy's voice was suddenly soft and conciliatory, catching Angie off guard. "Perhaps your elegant legs and my legendary needle were meant to work together."

Angie flushed with embarrassment and did a quick demi detourné to hide her blush. She couldn't think what to say.

Just then the cartographer came in and picked Gordy up from the map, fastening his trousers and pocketing him away. Angie was left staring flustered at the magnificent likeness of Gordy's needle drawn proudly on the map beneath her elegant silver legs. His needle certainly was legendary. Maybe he really was a compass after all.

The Day She Turned Away From the Mirror
By Anna Nymus

Her eyes were critics and her feet were still,
Far too long had she suppressed her will
To fulfill the idea and not the real thing;
She had been the kite, now she was the string.
The day came when the wind suddenly grew severe
And she swept across the daunting frontier,
Free from all manner of flamboyant expectation,
Knowing she wasn't built for long-standing pretension.
The glass could still see her, but she paid no mind
Staring into its depths can make a person go blind.
Despite being no danger in looking through the lens,
Fixated on the self, they are no longer friends.
It was the moment to explore the 'maybes';
With the timely help of a buoyant breeze
She breathed fresh beauty into the strains of her soul.
And so, a dancing diamond grew from a clouded coal.

Signed,
A Pictorial Poet

Fossilized
By Eliabeth Hawthorne

Metal clashed against metal as the blade glanced off the warrior's armor. The battlefield was stained with blood and the wind carried moans into the abyss of the deserted town. The dying were left to die with no one left to bury them. Angered by the drink it could not help but absorb, the earth decided to rebel. The fighting would end, one way or another. Just as the victorious warrior ran his blade through the wounded flesh of the other, they both turned into trees, locked together forever.

Vicious Tape
By Ermisenda Alvarez

I viciously threw the measuring tape to the ground. The black and white markings glared at me from down below. It felt good to throw it away. Why did I torture myself over a few kilograms or an inch? I didn't measure my relationships with my friends, my emotional state, or the breadth of my smile with a tape. So, why did I measure my self-image with one?

The tape appeared to writhe on the floor, wanting to latch onto my thighs, hips, and waist to criticize and ridicule me. I had come to realize that a healthy body cannot be determined by a black and white number. I ripped the tape in two. There were so many beautiful shades of grey and I was happy with mine.

Untitled
By Karyl Zshamaine

Strawberry curls flying in the wind…
Ring of daises 'round her lovely hair…
As she ran barefooted on emerald grass,
Her laughter filled the soft spring air.

White cotton dress blown by the breeze,
A little girl hiding behind the trees…
A yellow butterfly came in sight,
And her amethyst eyes shone with delight.

On the front porch she awakes from slumber,
Reality creeps in and she'd soon remember…
Those were but mem'ries of days long gone
Eaten by the cancer that brought her down.

Tears filled her pale violet eyes,
No longer a brilliant purple shade,
Along her hollow cheeks, a steady cascade…
Rosy tresses fell and shorn,
In its place, a 'kerchief worn.
All beauty was lost, she thought,
All that's left, a bittersweet dream…
Eternal oblivion she sought.

But a warm hand covered her cold frail one,
With love, gentle lavender eyes shone.

No longer tiny, a li'l more of a lady,
Was the little girl in her dream…
'twas at that moment that she understood,
Golden locks were not her crowning glory,
But her loving and caring family…
Circles 'round her eyes, hair cropped and trimmed,
She's more beautiful now than she had ever been.

So this is Christmas!
By D. Judy

So this is Christmas…

But what have you done?

That night I saw an angel fall from the sky. Her golden hair gradually lost its shine as she reached the ground. Her beautiful white gown was stained with dirt. I could not see her eyes or her face, but I knew that she was the loveliest thing that could ever exist on Earth. She looked so fragile and innocent.

So why? Why did you send her away from your kingdom up among the clouds and stars?

I was there. I saw the red petals falling like rain onto her body. It looked like a shower of blood. What has she done? What is her story?

I did not know what to do, but as an honorable man I felt it was the natural thing to go and help. I slowly walked towards her. She was immobile. Was she even breathing? I bent down and, with a trembling hand, I touched her blonde locks.

She moved.

She sat up and looked up at the sky. Then she looked at me.

I held my breath as she stared straight into my eyes and through my soul. Her eyes were like the infinite ocean and her skin was as fair and soft as a baby. Her voice was melodious, though a little broken as if it has been far too long since she had last uttered a word.

"Where am I?" she asked.

I opened my mouth and answered her with much effort. "In the forest of Azelga."

She stood up and looked around. I straightened up as well. "Who are you, fair lady? Are you an angel?"

The creature turned to me and smiled. She started to go round in circles and lifted her hands up in the air. Red petals fell onto her and her alone. She laughed as if I had asked her a stupid question.

This time when she spoke, it echoed everywhere. "Why do you say so?"

Then, something strange happened. The petals began to form a tornado around her; I could not see her anymore.

And it started to rain. For real. The water felt heavy upon my body. Soon, the red petals joined.

But as the petals touched me, they became blood.

Real dark blood.

I screamed but no sound came out of my mouth. The red substance covered my hair, my eyes, my skin. I could not move. I fell down. I could only smell the rusty odor of blood.

To my horror, my skin started to peel off. It burnt.

"Merry Christmas," the angelic voice cried out.

And she watched as I drowned in my own blood.

In Hope
By Anonymous at Korea, Love and Longing

This existence is nothing but the sound of the rain hitting the roof and a language you don't understand. Your life has been dismal and there is nothing you can do about changing the past. There is nothing to change the feelings of regret that you harbor. So you sit in agony and think about this very moment, where time feels like it's standing still. You find your beauty in broken pieces that equal something not worthy of love. When all you have to hold onto is the hope that tomorrow will fix what has been broken today.

Dangerous Waters
By Airicka Phoenix

"You can't tell anyone."

Mary looked down at her bare legs, speckled with sand. Droplets clung to the goose bump infested flesh. Unconsciously, her gaze darted to his legs. *So, normal now,* she mused. Long, toned, and speckled with golden hairs, tanned from hours beneath the sun. A pair of black swimming trunks hugged his trim waist. He hadn't pulled his t-shirt on, but Mary was more interested in his legs than the washboard abs and masculine torso.

"Would anyone believe me?" she murmured.

"No!" There was relief mingling with the annoyance stiffening his muscles.

She had to look away, had to focus on something else, anything else. So, she stared at the waves crashing over the sand, the sun setting over the horizon, and the spot he'd dragged her to after pulling her out of the water when her sides cramped up.

"You saved my life."

He shifted beside her but didn't comment.

Her gaze lifted to his, searching the face of her savior, a face crafted with angular features. Eyes the color of seaweed peered back at her from beneath crinkled brows. The sun shone through his hair like liquid gold over wet sand. He seemed so human. Had every pulse of heat washing off him not screamed with coiled panic, she could have easily chalked it all up to lack of oxygen, disorientation… a dream. But he was staring at her, practically begging her to forget, and she couldn't.

"I won't tell anyone," she whispered, needing to reassure him.

The shadow that dropped over his eyes, it was anger masking dread. "Why?"

It was an easy enough question to answer; because no one would believe her; because it sounded crazy even to her own mind; because she wasn't like that. Instead, she found herself replying, "Because you saved my life."

He seemed to absorb this a moment, searching her eyes as he did. Maybe the truth was hiding there or maybe he needed to believe her. He nodded slowly, getting to his feet.

"Wait!" she called before he could walk away. "What's your name?" she asked when he glanced back.

He hesitated, shifting from one leg to the other before answering, "Dylan."

Then, he was gone.

*

Mary dreamt of Dylan nightly for two solid weeks, tossing and turning against her sheets until they roped around her like snakes. It always happened the same way; she was swimming, pushing further and further from the shore, ignoring the slight pinch along her sides.

Below her, the open waters stretched like a black chasm threatening to swallow her whole. But in her dreams, she was never alone. He was always there, holding her when the pain in her stomach became too much and keeping afloat seemed impossible. But at the same time, it wasn't him at all. From the waist up, he was hard, golden muscles, square jaw and sandy tresses. But when he got closer, when he put his arms around her, drawing her into him, it wasn't skin she felt brushing her bare thighs. It wasn't even legs, but scales the opalescent shade of pearls beneath shimmering light.

She jolted from the deep sleep, damp with sweat, her heart crashing against her chest. The waves outside her window roared in her ears, seemingly mocking her for her weakness. She lay for what felt like hours, staring at the ceiling fan while the night whispered around her.

*

"What am I doing?" she groaned beneath her breath, clutching her purse straps tighter in her sweaty grasp. Was she really on the prowl for some guy she barely knew? The island just east of British Columbia's coastline was tiny, but it wasn't that tiny. For all she knew, Dylan was a tourist like her. He could have already left for the summer. What's more, he'd made it clear that he wanted her to stay away. Yet there she was, lying to her parents just so she could hunt him down.

Mary sighed, rolling her eyes heavenwards. This was crazy. She needed to get back to the hotel before her mother sent out a search party. Mary made the awful mistake of telling her mom about the near death experience; her mother had not been pleased that Mary could be so careless. It had taken a lot of fast talking to be allowed an hour on her own to go sightseeing, which she was using to find Dylan.

"Stupid," she muttered to herself, turning on her flats and starting back the way she'd come.

But halfway to the hotel, she found herself on the beach instead, sitting on the same rock she'd shared with Dylan, watching the ocean kiss the bank.

She was being irrational, becoming so obsessed with a stranger. She needed to forget him. Did it really make any sort of difference if she confronted him about it? Did it change the way she felt? It scared her that she wasn't there for that reason at all; she was there to see him.

"You came back."

Mary jumped, head snapping around to stare at the figure advancing on her from the left. "Dylan!" Her heart jumped in her chest. Her stomach fluttered. The unexpected jolt of excitement took her completely by surprise.

He stopped when there was three feet between them. "What are you doing here?"

"I wanted to thank you." It wasn't a complete lie.

His eyes seemed to narrow slightly, his head tipped to the side. "That's all?"

Mary slicked her lips, getting carefully to her feet. "No."

He sighed heavily, turning away. "You shouldn't be here."

"Wait!" She grabbed his arm before he could leave. "Are you...?"

The intensity behind his eyes bore straight into her soul. The taut stretch of muscle beneath her hand bunched.

"Please," she whispered when he continued to remain tight lipped.

"Would it matter?"

Would it? Would it make her run for the hills? Would it disgust her? It wasn't disgust that propelled her to take a step closer.

"No," she whispered without thinking — without

needing to think.

The rigid muscles along his shoulders slackened, seemingly melting like a cube of ice in the sun. The uncertainty and doubts lifted from his eyes and he smiled, exposing dimples on either side of his mouth. "I didn't ask you your name."

It was her turn to smile. "Mary."

Her Final Dance
By Tanitha Smith

The bullet hit her directly between her shoulder blades.

She arched her back, her head thrown back and her mouth open in a soundless scream.

Her shoulders snapped back unnaturally. Her arms bent the wrong way and her fingers splayed.

She tried to walk but her knees buckled. She rose up on tiptoe, silhouetted against the bright city standing tall and proud for the last time.

Her vision blurred. The yellow streetlights turned into floating circles, swimming in her foggy vision.

She fell slowly, her knees hitting the ground first, and then her stomach and her arms. Her head bounced once, and then was still.

A dark stain spread across her t-shirt. The cars roared by, their headlights flashing on her body. The noise of a thousand vehicles was deafening.

But not a single car stopped.

Wet Pages
By Melanie Coulthard

Words run from the page
Like red dye from a sock.
Separated from sentence and structure,
Evade recapture,
Reform to drift on tides
Of time and meter.
Metaphors slip through fingers
Land with splashes of delight
That ripples like a tidal wave in Lilliput.
If I were a poet,
I would immerse myself in such things.
Court charming nouns
Make art from recycled water drops.

Box Full of Doubt
By Eliabeth Hawthorne

Skeletons don't always stay in closets. No matter how hard you push the door closed, no matter how well hidden you kept them while you're alive, someone has to go through the closet when you die.

I found a box, a box full of doubt. It was not in your closet but under your bed, a box full of lies. Lies you told and I believed, things you said were lost or broken, things you said you mailed. What else did you lie about? Like a single loose thread that when pulled unravels the whole sweater, so my reality came unraveled and I began to doubt. How many of your stories were made up? It hurt to doubt you, especially because you're not here to explain it away.

Then I closed the box full of doubt. I can never close Pandora's box; I can never un-see what I saw. But, I can choose what I remember. I can choose to focus on the good memories, the cooking lessons, watching movies, listening to your stories. True or not, they are good memories, and focusing on the box will only taint them. It will only hurt me.

Untitled
By Gemini

Come for dinner this Sunday,
I will cook us up a feast:
Potatoes, peas and carrots,
A slice or two of beef.
I'm sorry Mum I can't.
Oh why? My dear mum said.
Mum, I tell you every week;
I can't eat something dead.
You can't eat something dead?
Don't be silly dear.
If it was still alive,
Mooing we would hear!
Anyway my love,
All you eat is dead.
The flour when it's ground
Is dead in your bread.
It started as a seed
As alive as you and me.
So don't be silly dear,
And eat the beef for me.

Blood Ties
By Ermisenda Alvarez

My aunt placed the tea on the table before exiting. These family reunions were always uncomfortable. The conversations grew hot, fast. Much more couldn't be expected from the grinding friction of personalities. I counted the hours until I would be home again.

Instead of fiddling with the hem of my shirt, I decided to drink the tea my aunt had offered me. She had a fascination with buying ornate plates, cutlery and cups. The intricate, golden design of the teacup winked at me. What disconcerted me was the content inside. Blood-red tea reflected my anxious expression. I took the teacup and rested the cool ceramic against my bottom lip.

I was only being paranoid. Right? This was normal tea. The sickly sweet liquid broke past the seal of my lips. I convinced myself the blood-red tea was a fitting choice for a family reunion. After all, wasn't it blood that forced us to converse this evening? One of us was going to inherit grandfather's estate and riches.

My hand flung to my throat, the teacup shattered. I couldn't breathe.

Which Witch?
By Anne Schilde

"Look, Mama! The trees are made of candy!" Annie stumbled along in tow, unable to match the pace of her mother's long strides.

"Quit dragging your feet, Annie. Can't you see it's getting late? The park closes at sunset."

"But they're made of candy!"

"Don't be ridiculous. It's just the autumn colors in the sunset, and that means it's getting late and the park will be closing soon."

Annie glued her eyes to the path as she tripped behind. There was no sign of cookie crumbs anywhere. Maybe the birds already got them.

"Do you think we'll see them?" she asked.

"See what?"

"Not what. Do you think we'll see Hansel and Gretel?"

"Why on Earth would we see Hansel and Gretel?"

"Because the trees are made of candy."

"Annie, you better learn to watch that imagination of yours. You've seen how much trouble it gets you into." She let go of Annie's hand, and slowed the pace a little to allow her daughter to keep up.

"Well, what about the witch?" Annie's voice was already trailing from a distance. "Will we see her?"

Her mother whirled to find Annie stooping to pick up a handful of leaves from the ground. "Flower Anne!" she shrieked, as the red leaves found their way to Annie's curious tongue. "Spit that out this instant!"

Annie spat the leaves out, not in obedience, but in disappointment. It certainly wasn't very good candy. Her mother snatched her hand again, pulling her too hard. She fell and skinned her knee, and then stumbled to her feet again to keep from being dragged.

"Will we?" she asked, trying to brush the stinging away from her knee with her free hand as she trotted to keep up.

"Will we what?"

"See the witch."

"Which witch is that?"

"The one with the gingerbread house."

"What did I tell you about your imagination?" She jerked harder on Annie's hand. "What makes you think there would be a witch now?"

"Because the trees are made of candy."

"I already explained, they are not made of candy."

"Well they look like candy."

"Hurry along." The irritation was really beginning to show in her mother's voice. "I don't know who puts these ideas in your head. There are no candy trees in Hansel and Gretel."

"Nuh, hu-uh, Miss Murray read…"

Her mother's hand stung her sharply on the cheek. "What have I told you about sass mouthing me, little Miss?"

Annie stood frozen, her eyes watery from the stinging. If she blinked, it would make tears, so she strained to keep her eyes open. Her mother didn't seem to care for the resulting expression, but she turned again and this time Annie followed along quietly. Her eyes darted back and forth in silence. There was a wicked witch in these woods. She could feel her evil, but maybe it wasn't the best thing to say so.

Untitled
By Kyllan Brindle

It had only been an hour since Mickey died and things just weren't going well. Here she was struggling to pick her limbs up, straining muscles in her neck and back. At least she thought she was. She couldn't quite remember what strain felt like, her ghostly form being free from physical limitations.

Death stood beside her clicking his tongue.

"Stop it," she said.

"Sorry." The clock, clock, clock noise ceased at once allowing the hum of the forest to return to the foreground.

Mickey's body had slumped forward and fallen, face first, into a pile of soggy leaves. Why was she out here again? What had she been doing?

"I'm really sorry about this."

"Shut up." Mickey didn't even give him a glance.

Death rubbed his neck with his left hand, his right maintaining a firm grip on his scythe.

Mickey sat in her own lap again. The skin was solid allowing her incorporeal form no purchase on her insides. The comforting enclosure of flesh and bone and blood was gone. She glared at Death.

"This is all your fault."

"I know. I said I was sorry."

The two just stared at each other for a long moment until Mickey forgot what she had been so angry about. Why was she wearing a dress? She put her thumb to her lip and nibbled at the end. She couldn't even bite her nail. It wasn't there anymore, not really.

Death put his hand on her shoulder. He let the scythe dangle down at his side.

"You looked beautiful in that dress, Mickey. I'm glad you wore it. It was my favorite. Very thoughtful of you. I only wish you could have made it a little further. See, I set a picnic basket up about a hundred yards from here. One hundred thirty-seven to be exact. I really thought we had something great going on. Now you're dead. I wish I could explain it."

He gave her a gentle push on the small of her back. Instinctively she started walking. Who was this man? What was he talking about? Who was that girl laying on the ground?

"I've been looking for love for I can't tell you how long. For some reason as soon as I start to get close to someone. And I mean really close to someone they... expire."

They stopped passing trees. Or more accurately, the trees ceased to be melting away into a muddy mixture of earthy colors that puddled behind them. It was like the world had been submerged in a mud bath and she was looking in from the outside. All around her white empty space stretched out into infinity. It was calm. Warm.

"I think we were on the verge of something great Mickey. But I guess that doesn't matter much anymore."

Death repositioned himself in front of her wielding the scythe in both hands now.

"I'm so very sorry," he said.

He hefted the scythe above his head.

"Find peace in this place, Mickey Edgerton. May you

find whatever sort of paradise it is that you are expecting."

He clenched the handles and brought it down. The edge was so fine that it cut reality itself as it passed through the air, allowing not even specks of dust or air opportunity to flee from the cutting edge that pierced the fabric of the universe.

"Wait," Mickey whispered. Death's supernatural reflexes paused the reaping tool inches from her throat. A flicker of recognition danced across her face and she frowned and knit her brow. She licked her lips before speaking again.

"Worst. Date. Ever."

Untitled
By Otheus

Haar handen glijden over de toetsen.
Geïnspireerd door het lugubere aangezicht
begint ze te spelen, meegevoerd door
de passie gaat ze verder voor
koude, kille, zwijgende toeschouwers
die ademloos luisteren, naar
het melodieuze spel van de dood.

Her hands are gliding over the keys.
Inspired by the ghastly view
she starts to play, carried away by
the passion, she continues playing for
the cold, chilly, silent spectators
who are listening breathlessly to
the melodic piece of death.

Twisted
By Eliabeth Hawthorne

What a show off. I thought about Lorelai Gilmore breaking her leg. "I took the blonde pretzel chick down with me," she explained to her mother, admitting she was, "too competitive for yoga." If only I could bring this woman down, but even the blonde pretzel chick was not at her level. Who shows up for yoga in high-heeled boots? Her figure was perfect, but something about the poses she did were disjointed and awkward. Her face was a blank canvas, not in pain, but not serene either. *Was she one of those rich people who moved mechanically through life without enjoying it?* Even though I envied her body, I did not envy her life.

Fallen
By Airicka Phoenix

They said I couldn't do it. They said that I was too afraid; as the new girl, the one from the city, I wouldn't have the guts to follow through. They said I was weak, pathetic, that my clothes were strange and my hair too ugly. They said I wasn't good enough unless I did it.

The flimsy railing creaked beneath my weight as I teetered, balancing between the heels of my feet and my toes. The wind lashed against me, as cruel and determined to kill me as the twisted faces behind me, watching. It snatched at my clothes, pushing and pulling, disrupting my balance.

I wasn't afraid! It wasn't even that high. If I could just ignore the bubbling in my stomach forcing itself up my throat, I'd actually have been able to open my eyes.

"Jump! Jump! Jump!" The chant grew louder and louder from the demons behind me.

Don't do it! The hoarse, frightened voice was in my head, the rational part of my brain battling to force logic into the jumbled chaos of my fears.

But it wasn't high! And the water didn't look too cold or deep. Besides, if I didn't… I would get laughed at for the rest of my life. No one would want to be my friend. I had to do it!

I had to!

Return of Memories Past
By Amber "Serene" Russell

The sight of her childhood summer home sent a shiver of grief through Mariette Holst. The swell of emotion that had begun within her chest at the airport was now proving to be more overwhelming than she had expected. She remembered the last time her family spent long summer days relaxing and playing at this very spot. She could even recall watching her father refurnish the building with his own two hands when she was a child; her mother had been so happy here, away from the terrible stress of the big city. She could feel the sting of threatening tears while looking at the building in this decrepit state, but instead of letting her emotions get the best of her, Mariette reached up and harshly rubbed her closed eyes to keep the tears at bay. Clenching her teeth, she marched forward, breaking away from her sister's protective arm around her shoulders. She didn't need to be sheltered anymore, not here and not after everything that happened.

Time had not been kind to the building by the sea; the salt water had all but torn the wooden structure apart. The vibrant red paint that the whole family had applied together was now completely gone and the wood underneath was slowly rotting away. Upon closer inspection, the two women could see that even the metal hinges upon the windows and door had rusted straight through.

"We shouldn't go inside. Let's wait for Jeremiah,"

Bretagne said loudly as she looked into a window. Mariette could tell that this was a hopeless journey; her parents had not traveled all the way to this island in decades, not since Reyna had died. Setting her jaw, she looked at her older sister defiantly, before she pulled on the door.

"I don't want to wait for Jeremy. You promised we would be gone before he even arrived and it's already past noon. I do not want to be here when the fishermen head back to the docks. You know how they can get." She dropped her voice at the last sentence, speaking through clenched teeth as she pressed the bottom of her boot to the door frame and pulled on the handle with all of her strength.

After several minutes, Mariette stopped and lowered her foot to the ground once more. She was no longer upset and feeling nostalgic about her childhood, instead she just wanted to get back to the town on the mainland and to her hotel room. Moving her leg back, she swiftly kicked the bottom of the door, much to her older sister's horror.

"Hey! Are you crazy? What are you doing? Calm yourself!"

Rushing over to her side, Bretagne grabbed Mariette by her shoulders and forced her to turn away from the door in time for Mariette's foot to connect with her leg. A sharp howl of pain escaped her lips and she shook her younger sister by the shoulders roughly.

"I knew I shouldn't have told you! Why did I let you come! You're going to bring the whole building down, you idiot!"

They were both shouting at each other now, the emotions finally getting the best of both women.

"I am not twelve Bretagne, you cannot tell me what to do anymore! I do not know why I even bothered to come; it is not worth spending time with you!"

She immediately regretted the words when they rang back into her ears, but she was unable to show remorse; her pride wouldn't allow such a sign of weakness. She could see the blow her words caused, but instead of addressing the anger, Mariette harshly jerked her shoulder from Bretagne's grasp and turned towards the building once more. It was then that both girls noticed that the door now stood ajar. Standing still, she could hear her sister draw in a sharp breath before taking a step towards the door and pulling it open wider. Everything remained inside from the last time she had been here, all the furniture, fixtures, even a few electronics. It appeared that her parents hadn't even had the strength nor heart to move anything out; instead they just boarded up the building without a second thought. As Mariette took a step forward, she could feel the muscles in her throat tighten dramatically.

"Reyna…" she whispered as she reached forward and picked up a small doll from the table next to the door. Her blue eyes found the grey pools of Bretagne as she showed her the ragdoll.

"If you cry, I fear I will not be able to keep myself composed," her older sister warned with a shaking voice.

Without saying another word, Mariette moved a pair of weather-beaten shoes out of her way, and moved further into the house. She couldn't bear to look at the Davenport sofa piled high with crumpled towels, sheets, and dirt. Like everything in the house, they were part of the last scene the inside of the building saw, the last scene that both sisters were part of decades ago. Bretagne's left hand covered her mouth as she moved towards the kitchen in the back of the house, pushing past her sister in order to reach the area. Mariette didn't bother to follow her. Instead, she made her way to the stairs that lead to the second floor, but thought better of walking on the rotting wood. She didn't want to fall through the ceiling and land back on the ground floor injured.

Instead, she decided to rummage through the fishing station near the living room. Her father and mother bought this stretch of land in order to fish and relax during the summer. Seeing all the equipment reminded her how much her father had given up after Reyna's accident. As she ran her finger along the dust on a fishing pole, she finally let her mind drift back to the last day her mother had been happy. All four of the children had been playing in front of the fishing cabin, their mother in a chair by the door looking out over the water at the harbor. If she had been paying attention to the children, the accident could've been avoided, but instead she had her nose buried in a book as the gentle sea breeze washed over the area. It was Reyna's turn in hide and seek, and though she was the youngest, the older kids insisted on cheating and picking the most difficult places to hide. No one witnessed the seven year old slip from the rickety bridge into the waves below. In fact, it wasn't until the silence caused their father to emerge from his fishing station inside that anyone noticed the young girl floating in the water.

Everyone heard his shouts at once and came out of the hiding spot or put down the book in order to understand what had happened. He had rushed Reyna inside to the couch and attempted to revive her as their mother brought down towels to dry them off. It soon became apparent that she had been in the water too long and could no longer be revived. Her father had still hurried Reyna to a hospital while their mother packed up their belongings; they were going to stay in town closer to the hospital. It had all happened so fast and Mariette had only been nine. She replayed that day over and over again in her mind since it had happened, but there were so many things she had missed that none of it added up. Bretagne's voice cut through her thoughts and broke the silence.

"Marie! I found them! We can go now."

Pressing her lips together, she looked around at everything once more.

"Alright, did you get all of them? Let me see."

Turning towards the kitchen, Mariette found her sister scooping up a large stack of papers into her arms and nodding her head towards the stack of books on the table.

"Will you please carry those; I cannot take everything on my own."

Gathering up the dust covered books in her arms Mariette let her sister lead the way out of the house and into the bright sunlight. Just before she left the building, she picked the doll up from the table by the door and stepped onto the stone path outside.

Turning, she pulled the door closed tightly, and then closed the rusted metal screen. "I think I am going to come back next week." She said a bit too quietly, though she knew her sister heard her.

"What?" Bretagne asked, shocked at the confession.

"Yes. I think I will come and collect more things, perhaps explore this place and see what else I can find."

The older woman paused, took a deep breath, and

looked out over the water towards the docks on the mainland.

"Yeah, that sounds like a good idea, do you mind if I join you?" Smiling softly, she looked back at her younger sister. "Would it be so bad if Jeremy joins us, too?"

Pausing in thought, Mariette let a smile cross her face as well.

"No I suppose not. He can tell us all about his recent divorce."

Both of the women chuckled all the way to the bridge where they grew somber again. Pausing for a moment, Mariette tossed the doll she was holding into the water and watched it float away into the sea, where it belonged.

Red Fibers of Her Being
By Anonymous

The fibers of her red, golden, brown and beautiful locks are alive with promise. The light reflecting on each strand makes her more beautiful than I'd ever imagined. The sun is bright and hurts my eyes and skin, but she does not feel it. Her limp body has received the harsh punishment life has inflicted upon her too many times. Now, she is defeated. She does not fight back, she never fights back. The terrible irony of life that emanates from her hair, rich with color. Waves crash against the dead wood she lays upon, and we remember her just as we see her.

Arachnid
By Ermisenda Alvarez

Itsy bitsy spider. I had to collect the same spider again, and again; the spider with the dotted back and tiger-striped legs. I wasn't sure why the grand Countess of our kingdom required so many.

Once I collected the spiders required, I returned back to the palace of the Countess. As I walked to the cages, something caught my eye. People bustled about in the next room. Curiosity gripped me and I peeked within.

The Countess was draped in the most dazzling, exotic, and haunting gown I'd ever witnessed. The dress was inky black, spotted with starry-white flecks. Her sleeves and neckline were adorned with what appeared to be ribbons of obsidian and honey-gold. My jaw dropped at the splendor of the design. The colors shifted like a kaleidoscope.

Suddenly, I started to feel sick. The web of doubt tangled my thoughts, made my throat sticky, and my stomach heavy. Realization clenched my heart with eight legs. I dropped the cage. Dozens of itsy bitsy spiders ran towards the Countess. The dress… it… it was writhing.

The Puppet Master
By Stephanie Ayers

"That circus tiger is going to break your heart," Finn said to Abigail as he cleaned the puppets and tightened the screws of their joints.

Abigail, absorbed in counting their profit, ignored him.

"You can't take something that wild and turn it to paper."

"Hmmm?"

She did not look up from the bills spread out before her. Neat stacks of currency lined the small wooden table according to value.

"Nothing."

He shook his head. Everything he said was important, but she only listened when she wanted to.

"You said something about turning something wild into paper..."

She turned her head slightly. The circus car they shared was small. It consisted of two tables, a dresser, and a bed. A nudge of her elbow would send him sprawling to the floor.

"Yeah, I did. I was just musing."

He laid the last puppet into the wooden box where they slept between shows. So far, every show had been successful. No one in the world had puppets as life-like as theirs. People turned out by the dozens to see them. He still worried about what would happen if the police stopped by asking for their permit. They had none, but did the show for profit anyway. The rising popularity of the show brought the reality of fines and possible jail time closer to home. Abigail would never survive in jail.

"Well, stop. You aren't making any sense. Besides, I need a neck massage. You know how badly it hurts after a show. Stop playing with the puppets and give me a massage!" She packed the money tightly in an envelope and closed the safe.

She always demanded, never asked, and he always obliged. He did so now, begrudgingly. The circus tiger was still on his mind. So very wild it was and Abigail wanted to put its likeness on paper and use it as a background for a show. The whole circus scheme, hiring them for their unusual puppet show, made him uncomfortable, though it did provide a cover. He stopped massaging, running his hand through her long mahogany hair.

"So, did we do it? Do we have enough?"

She turned on her stool, one smooth leg crossing and uncrossing until she faced him. He was a handsome man with his clean cut golden brown hair, lean shape, and dimpled smile.

"No, not tonight, but it was close."

He slammed his fist on the table.

"Dammit, Abby!" His eyes wandered over to the puppet box. He moved to it swiftly and pulled out two puppets. They were new, a green genie and the red-faced butcher.

"And yet, you buy more puppets!"

Spittle landed on Abigail's face. She flicked it off with the back of her hand.

"Yes! New puppets that will make us even more money, Finn!"

Finn shook the puppets, squeezing the butcher hard enough to break him.

"Wonderful! Just what we needed!"

Sarcasm dripped from his lips.

"Tell me, exactly how did you plan to fit a genie and a fat old butcher into the show? Were you going to wish for a pig?"

Abigail shrunk back, away from the fist she expected to plow into her body at any moment. Anger always got the better of Finn. It would not be the first time a bruise had marred her porcelain flesh.

"Yes, we will grant the audience three wishes! What a great idea!"

She shook as her hands clasped together with excitement she did not feel.

"You'll see! The money will come rolling in! Then we can leave. We'll go wherever you want!"

Finn cooled down. She knew how to defuse his anger, though it did not always work.

"Three wishes, eh? So how do we go about making the wishes come true unless we know about them beforehand?"

Silence pierced the tension in the room. Abigail knew exactly how to get the three wishes fulfilled. Her grandmother taught her well. Finn never knew where the puppets came from, never questioned until now.

Finn set about fixing the broken puppet, something he always did when he needed to think.

"I have an idea, Finn," Abigail interrupted. Finn ignored her long enough to lay the butcher down delicately.

"What is that, Abby?" His eyes rolled sideways to look

at her.

"We could set up three people in the audience, each holding a slip of paper with the wish we want them to share. Then, we write the story to follow and make them come true."

Finn's jaw dropped open. It was a clever idea, one that would suit all purposes. She kept her face devoid of emotion as she waited for his response. He started to speak, stopped, examined the puppet again, tightened a screw, and stopped, then repeated the whole process once more before answering.

"You know, I do think that would work. Can we trust three people to play along?"

"Yes. I know three who would be willing."

Abigail smiled. She knew exactly who would play along and why.

"Excellent. I'll start writing the script for tomorrow then." Finn turned to the map of the world stretched across the wall behind him. Abigail knew he was looking for where he wanted to go. She would make sure he got there.

"Did you decide where we are going next?" she asked.

"Hmmm. I want to go somewhere exotic, but our funds, even if this is successful, won't allow for that. We need to move from here though before the police catch on to us. What do you think of Niagara Falls?"

She smiled again. "Sounds like a plan!"

*

Abigail peeked over the top of the stage. As expected, today brought a larger audience than ever before. She spied her three minions and, when they returned her look, shot them the evil eye. They shivered to her satisfaction.

Finn finished his lines and Abigail dropped the genie on the stage.

"Who dares summon me from my sleep?" the genie asked.

"It is I, the lonely butcher!"

The genie's large green eyes rolled in extreme exaggeration.

"Humph. Fine. I grant you three wishes. What shall they be?"

Glitter sprinkled onto the stage.

"Who among you knows my plight?" the butcher asked.

He pointed to the audience. A female voice shouted from the crowd, "I wish for a new home away from these others!"

"So shall it be!" the genie answered. She waved her wand and glitter filled the stage.

A puppet sized box appeared in front of her. "I don't have time for games, now. On with your second wish or I'll feed you to the tiger!'"

Another female voice, older this time, trembled as it voiced, "I wish to be thin and handsome!"

The genie waved her wand again and glitter fell over the butcher. When it cleared, a leaner, younger butcher resembling Finn stood where the old fat one had been. The genie blew a wolf whistle. "Hello, thin and handsome! Starve the tiger and tell me your third wish?"

A male voice boomed from the audience, "I wish I was a puppet master!"

Another wave of glitter filled the stage, and miniature puppets lined up in front of the butcher. "There, you are a puppet master!"

*

Abigail hummed as she cleaned the puppets and placed them gently in their box. She opened the new box and pulled the puppet out. She brushed the clean cut golden brown hair until it gleamed, then ran her finger down the lean body. She fingered the label postmarked for Niagara Falls glued to the front of the box. She sighed. A hint of a smile creased her face as she placed him inside the box.

"If I loved you, that's my fault. Now, it's time to let you go," she said as she placed one circus tiger stamp on the box after another.

Girls Can Fly!
By Anonymous

When the memories came, they tore at her stomach with icy fingers and hijacked her mind. It didn't matter if she was hunched over a keyboard, or in a green room preparing for a TV appearance. The terror would suck her into the seedy, addiction fueled violence that was her youth. A time when her mother lived in the bottom of a bottle and her father, who refused to admit he was part of the problem, expected her to care for the house and her mother. If she failed to meet his standards, she was rewarded with cigarette burns and beatings. She was ten when one of his lessons left her bleeding, with loose teeth and a broken rib on the bathroom floor.

Huddled on the bed, she waited for him to pass out before slipping out the window. Wracked with pain, she made her way to the local hospital; after that, things got blurry. Confusion reigned as they tried to find her parents and more importantly, who would pay the bill. Eventually they called a social worker, who, after one look at the battered girl, set the wheels in motion to secure a better life for her.

Reluctant at first and afraid of her father's reaction, she begged them to let her go home, but her mentor refused, eventually making her see that her parents needed help and that what was good for her was not one of their priorities. After bouncing in and out of a few foster homes, she met her new parents and discovered a talent for writing that they encouraged. Over the years, her body healed, but her mind wore Band-Aids, ready to fall off at any time.

Now, she was a successful author. Two of her books had been adapted for the big screen and she was working on a Broadway play. At the age of thirty-three, she met a man who just may be the one she would grow old with. She had money, a great house, and a few friends she could count on. Life was good. Her mother died years earlier, but her father tried to make contact a few times, hoping to cash in on her fame and fortune. She ignored him.

Jumping as the intercom sprung to life, instructing her to head to the set, she thought about her organization and the kids and women it would help. Vowing to get as many of them out of violent situations as she could, she took a deep breath and headed to the stage to sell her latest book, the one with fifty percent of the proceeds going to the "Kids First" organization. She rose from the ashes, now it was time to help others fly!

Better than a Yellow Brick Road
By Eliabeth Hawthorne

Pop. My neon glasses protected my eyes from the blast of colored powder, but the rest of my face now shimmered in a green even Envy would be jealous of. Impatient children rolled through the colored puddles and fairies fluttered about in pinks, orange, and white. Color fell from my cupped hands as we waited for the countdown. 3... 2... 1... Throwing the dust into the air, we were engulfed in a rainbow cloud that settled on the brick beneath our feet. My painted nails and red lipstick no longer looked out of place. To us, the colored powder brought out a childish glee as if at any moment it would pick us off the path we ran and carry us to Neverland. For others, it had the power to grant wishes.

Dear in the Headlights
By Anne Schilde

Maggie stumbled through the field, mumbling to herself as she recounted the night's events. Graduation night. It was supposed to be the biggest night of her life— the night before the first day of the rest of her life.

Graduation was everything it was supposed to be, except for the parts that came before and after the ceremony itself. Her father never showed and he didn't answer his phone. The text from Lyssa that came mid-commencement wasn't helpful.

Out with IT. Should be here??

Maggie had smiled when it came, thinking back to her older sister's texts before the advent of auto-correct. "IT" meant their father's new girlfriend, Carol. Lyssa hated her. Lyssa didn't have to live with her. Carol really wasn't all that bad, except for the cocaine, and the booze, and her immature tantrums, and of course her father's absence on just the biggest night of her life. At the end of the ceremony he still wasn't there.

Lyssa offered to drive her home, but she was turned down. Everyone who was anyone was going to a big graduation party at Raven's Nook. Steve was going and so Maggie was going. She was already dressed for it under her gown.

Steve said he wanted to talk.... alone. They found a private place. He fumbled with his words for an awkward minute before getting on one knee in front of her. The finality of a childhood that was gone, the love of a young man, the magnitude of responsibility of life and of challenges… The racing pulse in her ears made it hard to hear, but Steve still wasn't finding the right words anyway and then they were interrupted by Myra, Steve's ex-girlfriend, who insisted she had to talk to him.

"I'll bring him right back," Myra said, as she dragged him away by his shirt.

Maggie sat down. Anger filled her with more adrenaline than her interrupted proposal had. *He was going to propose, right? Why else would he get down on a knee? Myra knew it, too. That bitch!* She wanted to chase after Myra and tear her hair out, an ironic desire as it would turn out. Instead, she sat. Someone handed her a drink. She thought it was Jeff, Steve's best friend, and she absent-mindedly accepted it. The next hours were a blur.

She was alone with Scott – *Oh God. Why Scott?* – conscious enough to keep pushing off his advances, but unable to stop the onslaught of alcoholic kisses and groping under her clothes. On the plus side, she barely remembered it and he didn't rape her. At least she didn't think so. She was still dressed.

Later, there were some really bright lights and she was sure she remembered Myra's face and her hideous laugh. That was most likely when her hair disappeared. *I hope that bitch doesn't think she can get away with this just because school's out!*

When she finally passed out, she was alone. She had managed to get away from everyone and find her way outside where the hyperventilation of fresh air sent her pitching face first to the ground. When she woke up, the noise from the party had died down some and she was wrapped in Steve's jacket. *Why would he just leave me lying like this?*

It was more than two miles down the cliff beneath Raven's Nook and out across the fields. That was at least a mile and a half shorter than walking the road that wound down the back side of the hill and a hundred percent less likely to produce company. The summer weeds tore at her ankles. The warm breeze felt strange where her hair had been chopped away. Finally, she could see the highway ahead in the dark, the road home.

Home. She wasn't even sure she wanted to go home. *Why didn't he come to my graduation?* She began to cry. Softly at first, but little by little, the frustrations of the evening poured themselves down her face. Her sobs were interrupted by the sound of a lone car on the highway, freezing her in her tracks. She didn't want to see anyone. She didn't want anyone to see her. She would wait for it to pass.

When the headlights came flying through the air, as the car hurtled over the embankment, Maggie could only stare blindly into them. They were so unnatural. *Cars don't fly.* But this one did. It came straight at her, an eerie invader from outer space, hovering toward her in slow motion, the lights blurred into duplication by her tears, engine screaming with no ground to restrict the wheels. Her mind couldn't process what she saw and heard, only the cool sting of her cheeks drying in the warm summer night air.

Vehicular manslaughter.
Reckless driving.
Driving under the influence.
Possession of narcotics.
As he lay in the hospital bed, alone with his thoughts,

none of those charges could mean a thing compared to the
crime that had no punishment. The driver's girlfriend was
dead. Fraught with grief, he knew that if her head hadn't
been in his lap when the car went off the road, the airbag
wouldn't have snapped her neck. And the poor girl he saw
right before the crash. They said she died instantly. *Good
God! What was she doing in that field?* But it was the
unpunished crime that would haunt him far longer than
the others. He knew it was that crime that caused them all.
If he had just taken Carol to his daughter's graduation,
none of this could have happened.

Untitled
By Samantha Warren

Deanna sat on the edge of the hard, straight-backed chair, her short fingernails digging into the wood underneath as she gripped the seat. She kept her eyes locked on the cup in front of her, watching the red liquid swirl in the small porcelain mug. The queen sat across from her, black orbs dancing with delight at the girl's discomfort. Her cruel lips curled in amusement. Deanna blinked and met the hard stare. Straightening her shoulders, she told herself to be brave. Her fingers curled around the small handle, lifting the deadly liquid to her lips. Her fear faded as she drank.

The Simplicity of Snowflakes
By Tanitha Smith

The snowflakes swirled peacefully, clean and white against the coal-black sky. All was silent. I just let myself stand there, drinking in the simplicity of falling snow. I stood as still as an ice sculpture, just watching and admiring as the world became white.

Gradually, the dirty yellow slush was covered up, washed blank, made new. Churned mud slowly disappeared under the soothing hand of snow; fresh, remade. Dirty grass, dying plants, naked trees, all were washed clean by the pure snowflakes. Everything was an innocent white.

As I watched the world being rewritten, I felt an odd sort of peace. A peace that had been desperately lacking from my life. It was as if the snow was rewriting _me_, as well as my surroundings. The entire past year, with all its disappointments and resentments and arguments... all those terrible things, the guilt that weighed me down, broke my spirit... that was behind me now. It was in the past, no longer a part of me. The softly falling snowflakes were scrubbing the pain of the past from my soul.

The sensation of peace grew, strengthening my limbs. I felt a vigor I hadn't felt in years. A new year. A new start. A new beginning for myself. The snow would wash away my sins and I could start again. Build a new life.

I will make my next year a _happy new year_.

Little Red Riding Hood
By Ermisenda Alvarez

The wolf stared at her. She stared at him. She wanted to look away—she didn't want to entice him—but she couldn't.

The cookies weighed her down like an anchor. Her heart threatened to burst. The wolf took a step forward. The basket of baked goods fell from her limp fingers, and the cookies scattered across the grass.

Without hesitation, she ran in the opposite direction. The deep dark forest was only meters away. Maybe she could lose him among the trees. The branches tore at her skin and whipped her face. Shreds of her ruby red dress dripped from the trees' branches. She glanced behind her. The wolf was out of sight.

She'd strayed from the path. Her mother's cookies for her grandmother were spoiled. The weight of guilt flooded her eyes with tears. She had to find her way back home. Just as she turned around, she came face to face with the wolf: a man.

Sunday Girl
By Devina S.

We both lay beside each other in contented silence, backs on the sun-warmed tier boards. Her eyes to the sky and the sky in her eyes. Mine were on her. They couldn't help themselves as her flaming coppery locks stirred lazily by the cool salty breeze. Not for the first time I wondered, but I dared not ask, *why me?* I was nothing special, anything but. Paperboy in the dawn shivering my behind off in the biting morning mist, community college during the day and gas station attendant at night.

Not enough sleep but I had to scrape by on what I save up. So that I could run. Run away from the sneering privileged clowns who feel as if they own the very dirt you walk on because their daddies were rich. Run away from the indignity of being born of… of… I swallowed, no I mustn't go there. Time with this stunning, living, breathing enigma was to be treasured, not be wasted on dark, useless thoughts. She was my enigma, no one else's. I smiled to myself. A secret I held close to my heart. But then she had secrets of her own as well; one of them I came close to understanding this very morning. The discovery chilled me to the tips of my toes.

"A penny for your thoughts," she said softly, a chime really, looking straight at me for God knows how long. I had been staring at her, but not looking, but she saw. Oh, this woman saw everything it seemed.

"Stray thoughts. Nothing really."

"But you looked angry… and sad, then you were smiling. Come on now, tell me, you always tell me everything." She pouted her full pink lips but she got serious. "You're not bipolar are you?"

God, she was beautiful. I laughed, but my throat burned.

"No, I'm not. It's… it's just things I remember, things I can't even speak aloud by myself. I can't, but I tried so many times in my head to tell you, but the words always come out wrong …" I trailed off. *And I'm scared to death you'll never come back,* I left unspoken.

"Oh." Her green cat's eyes were sunbeams that shone with warmth through my soul, or what I felt was my soul. It's a silly notion, but it was nice to have such intense attention focused on me by anyone, but especially by her, the Sunday Girl.

It's true what she'd said, well not everything, but I told her a lot about me and I never in my twenty years could I believe I'd share so much with another human being albeit a strange one. Maybe that was why: because she was so different from anyone I'd ever met. Generally with people you can clump them together and label them as uncaring, pretentious, sincere, well-intentioned, etc., not exactly stereotypes, but they all have a similar bearing.

But my Sunday Girl, she'd listen and not say anything until I finished. She'd take my words that were floating in the air between her fingers one by one and look at them and then look at me with a soft gaze, one I had prayed that she never show to another man. Then she'd tell me what she thought. Somehow she's always found a way to make my faults seem less of a burden and more like little odd gifts that only I had. And like now, she'll only push so far to get me talking and let me be if I wouldn't. She didn't judge me, just accepted. That was why I find it hard to believe she even exists at all.

But this wasn't the only bit that puzzles me about her, there was something much more strange. Sunday Girl only showed herself to the sleepy mazes of Trinton on Sundays; that's where she got the name but I knew her real one. No one has seen her on any other day of the week, even me. The one time I'd ask where she came from, she became distant and only said, "Oh, just somewhere far from here." I never asked again.

When I finally save up enough money and graduate, that being not long from now, I wonder if she'll meet me again where ever I'll be by then. It scares me that we mightn't. What if I don't leave after all? What if I stay in this damned town just for her? Would we even have a future or will I succumb to her spell and wait for her every Sunday of my life onwards?

Someday I'll build enough courage to ask her all these and more, but as I now stand here on the roof of my house overlooking the bay an hour after we parted once again. I just looked. Looked at her silhouette against the fading sun as she perched on the end of the pier boards, as she extended a long shapely leg, letting her toes skim the high water and step onto the surface as if she's walking on the ground. I just looked as she descended into the gently lapping waves blazing with the colors of the sunset. And looked as her fiery hair disappeared into the depths from which she came each time, each Sunday, the day I only lived to see.

A New Mask
By Anna Nymus

In his case, the step off the ledge was a bullet, soon to be embedded in his brain. Torn between wanting to live this life and leave it, he knew that whichever side he chose, the other side would lurk.

Day and night, he wore a mask of light, although the darkness was as much a part of him as the other. The shadows that played in the dark sometimes too closely resembled the rays of light, until he was left not knowing what his reasons were to stay.

To shed the mask, he searched for a way. But, was forced to explain himself at every turn—the whys and hows of his behavior. Though he hurt no one, no one but himself.

He hesitantly put away the trigger and summoned his demons. They stared him in the face as he gave them a good hard look. They weren't a danger to him as long as he watched them, he realized. He knew there was only one way they would never leave his sight. After a long thought, he decided they would make up his new mask.

They would be his shield and his strength. There would be no more expectation of light, and if it did sneak in, he would enjoy it. But for now he'd enjoy the dark. It meant something different to him than to others, he finally admitted.

After that, he never saw another day. Only the night.
And something about it just felt right.

Signed,
A Fellow Goth

Separated by Seasons
By Eliabeth Hawthorne

Red curls cascaded whimsically around her as though she were a mermaid come to meet me on the docks. Sometimes it felt that way actually. She had vivid green eyes that always danced with light, as though reflecting the stars even in the middle of the day. During the summer, we were inseparable; her family rented a house on the lake next to ours, but the rest of the year she was far away. I liked to imagine she was under the ice, just as anxious to come back into my world as I was to have her there. When I went skating, I would pretend she swam under me, keeping pace with my blades. Did she think of me the same way?

Neverland
By Marisa Lyon

"Wow, this one's heavy," she grumbled, placing the box on the flimsy wood beam. "Cleaning out the attic, what a glamorous way to spend a Sunday morning." Her cranky expression mocked.

The raindrops splashed against the window. The wind howled through the creases. The dreary gray sky mirrored her disposition.

BOOM!

The startling crack of thunder echoed through the old house, rattling its bones and uncontrollably sending a mess of blonde hair and contorted legs to the attic floor.

She soothed her now throbbing head and scraped knee, as the swinging light bulb flickered a few times before going black. Only a hazy ray of light peeked through the window and across the room, illuminating the dusty path.

"Figures," she griped.

That's when she saw it. A tall, curvy bottle at the end of the dim stream slowly came into focus, as her eyes and pounding head adjusted. She inquisitively crawled to it, popped open the top, and turned it over.

The tiny, sand-like crystals slipped through her fingertips, reflecting shimmers of color off her face. Wide-eyed, mouth agape, she watched the pixie dust dance through the air and swirl around her. The colorful gems radiated a bright light as they circled, forcing her eyes shut.

When the glow dimmed, she opened them to

unimaginable enchantment.

It was truly a dream world, somewhere in between being asleep and awake. The forest echoed with song. The sun beamed and the air tickled her skin. She took a cautious step upon the supple earth. It was like nothing she had ever experienced, yet there was a recognizable element in everything, from the feel of the ground beneath her to the sound of the waterfall in the distance.

She hesitantly spun around, taking a second account of her surroundings before springing toward the gleaming falls. She climbed over rocks soft as cardboard that lined the path, before reaching the cool, crisp water and plunged her hands into the cascade.

A familiar crack boomed in the distance although she couldn't place its sound. It wasn't startling, but rather pleasant, as if nature was speaking to her. She pranced along a short path to the clearing, and peered down the stair-like slope. A sun-drenched valley led to a colorful lagoon sparkling below.

She smiled, twirling around, breathing in the wondrous life surrounding her. It was beautiful, but she couldn't shake the feel of familiarity: familiar yet sweeter. Was it a place she had once dreamed of?

Perhaps the daydream she often longed for, an escape from her ordinary life. But it was never like this. This vibrant world was special. Sacred. And she was special for being a part of it. Why had it been hiding all this time? Or was it somewhat here all along? She couldn't be sure. But she had found it now, and was never letting go.

Fire on Fingers
By Lee-Anne

Ancient memories stirred within my heart. The world blurred and ran like colors in the rain. Deep within I felt the call of the universe. I felt it burn and coil through my being. Suddenly, without warning, the fire leapt to my fingertips as it scorched through my being, called there by some ancient connection to a long lost world.

"Uriel, my fire." The words whispered through my veins. "Uriel, it is time to remember."

My cloak fell away as wings sprouted from my spine. Before me the world shrank away, beneath me the soil glowed as fire engulfed my being.

People shrank away from me, the heavens opened above connected with Earth through the pillar of fire I had become. With a mighty heave, I lifted away from Earth and rejoined the light.

"Home," sighed my being.

"Uriel," whispered the light.

"Uriel," shouted the masses.

"I am Uriel, Fire of God, and these are my memories. You are my chosen channel to write my words." The words flow from angel to me.

As I type, the fire floods through my veins and lights my keyboard. As it burns my resistance away I feel the power of Uriel merge with my own small being.

What am I? Who am I? What am I becoming?

Run for Your Life
By Jenny Tacken

I run, barefoot across the tentacles of icy grass blades across the Moors.

My hair laces its way into the air so cold it could freeze me in time.

My heartbeat skips, vapored breath escapes my mouth. I try desperately to hold the air in my lungs.

They won't capture me, they won't get me … they won't.

My life depends on my speed. The fog is settling, night is drawing in. Soon it will be dark. I need to see the way before me. *Please give me more time, PLEASE I beg, do not let darkness fall.*

I struggle to catch my breath, my lips are so cold, my mouth is parched.

God… NO, a storm is brewing, run, don't you look back Esmay, don't you dare.

The thorns stab at my feet; it hurts with every step I take. Don't cry, don't cry.

Erase the pain Esmay, erase it now!

I push myself, no time to dwell on how my body aches. It is so cold, I am so tired, but I must not give in.

I am the hunted, being chased down like foxes that chase their frightened prey.

How much more can I take, I'm struggling. How can I continue, how can I break free? How do I outrun them?

"Please don't let the storm come, PLEASE!" I yell to

the emptiness around me. I don't have the strength inside me to also battle rain. *How much more can I take?*

I am so scared and long for home, to warm myself in front of the fire with the door locked fast.

I hear them, the horses' hooves resonate through the ground underneath me.

Don't look back, my thoughts echo in my head. There is no time to see how close they are.

You will not get me, you will not lock me up again.

I swear you will not imprison my soul once more.

Opposing Forces
By Ermisenda Alvarez

To and fro we danced. Sensual twirls, abrupt dives. It was easy at first. The ground was arid like a desert, my toes dry. With each lock of our gazes, I found myself closer to him. My eyes lost their flirtatious flutter. I tugged to free myself. While his form was gentle, a strength that intimidated me lay quietly beneath the surface. I despised him. The two of us could never work.

From the frantic and energetic moves we started from, we had surrendered to rhythmic swaying. The tension dissipated as waves of chemistry swirled around us. His body molded around mine. We were alone in an ocean of intimacy; wet fingers touched moist tongues. I felt safe. My leg encircled him; ripples of pleasure ran up my thighs. They often say love and lust are enemies, but why not lovers?

Sisters
By AR Neal

It was Mama and Sister's favorite dress. Gramma had made it for my confirmation and everyone—especially Mama and Sister—thought I looked like an angel in it, even though it was really too big then. I am glad they got to see me in it for confirmation because they smiled like they were really happy; they weren't happy often. It's been two years and I try not to think too hard about them anymore, not since the accident. I didn't mean to, that is to say, I didn't want it to happen.

I love the mirror in the attic. I always have. It used to seem so much bigger, but now it's just right. Gramma keeps the dress up here now instead of in the back bedroom closet; she says it reminds her of Mama and Sister too much. I don't get that since it's my dress. Anyway, I started coming up here a lot after I came to live with her all the time. She doesn't like that I come up here, but I don't care. She spends so much time crying in her lace hankies that she doesn't pay much attention to me anyway.

I used to pretend that the mirror was magic. It seemed like, instead of a reflection of the attic, it was a whole different place in there. One time when I was playing tea party, I smiled at my reflection and it didn't smile back. The me in the mirror looked so sad. I asked her if she wanted to play with me and that's when she smiled. I was so excited I brought Sister up here to show her, but instead of smiling, the me in the mirror grabbed Sister and dragged her into the mirror. I couldn't believe it so I went and got Mama and the same thing happened to her. I told Gramma but she wouldn't come up to see; instead, she mumbled something, spit into the dust at the bottom of the attic steps, used that funny key to lock the attic door, and tried to get me to stay out. I say 'try' because I could get the door open with a hairpin and the first time I came up, I saw she had covered up the mirror. Gramma didn't say anything to anyone for a while and after the first good snow made up a story about Mama and Sister and the lake. I didn't want to get in any trouble so I stayed out of the attic for a while, but I figured the me in the mirror would be lonely, so I came back. By then, Gramma didn't seem to care what I did. I found the dress up here too; Gramma had just thrown it in an old brown paper shopping bag. That hurt my feelings and it made the me in the mirror sad too. I could tell because she got really happy when I took it out of the bag, shook it out, and put it on. I liked her; it was like having a twin sister, which sort of made up for what happened. It made me feel not so lonely.

I liked having someone to really play tea party and dress-up with and the me in the mirror could do tricks. She could make more copies of herself, or of me, or however you want to think of it. I told my friend Polly at school, but I told her like it was sort of a made-up story. Polly said I was strange and then she stopped being my friend. I came home and went straight to the attic. For the first time, the me in the mirror came out. She smiled at me and danced with me while the others stayed on the other side and danced with us. I've decided I want to stay here with them. They never make me cry, they don't think I'm strange, and I know if someday I go with them I'll be with Mama and Sister again. For now, I've made some sandwiches and locked myself in here. I guess Gramma will eventually try to come and get me, but I know my new sisters will take care of me.

Untitled
By Terry Shepherd

Dressed in white
Pure as gold,
Waiting for him,
His hand to hold.
Chairs are placed,
Filled up with people.
Music playing in the background,
People gazing all around.
Flowers scented the air,
Petals lying on the floor,
Minister standing in front to see.
Family is wondering what has happened to her.
Vows were practiced,
Rehearsals were done.
Wedding party standing in place,
Tears are streaming down her face.
The groomsmen were nowhere to be seen,
The spot where he should stand now empty air.
She had been stood up by the groom who had nothing to
say.
The marriage unspoken, the two parted ways.

The Shortcut
By Kyllan Brindle

The shoulder of the highway was where the two boys stopped. A lonely howl swam through the air around them, drifting over tree tops, across the road, and into somewhere beyond.

"I don't like the sound of that," said the first.

He pulled the straps on his backpack tighter.

"Me neither," said the second. "It's getting dark. And it's time for dinner already."

A pair of headlights drifted around the corner and floated past them, a white mechanical steed ushering someone else toward home.

"We could take a shortcut."

"You don't know any shortcuts," said the first. "Of course I do. I know these woods like the back of my hand." And with that, the second burst into the tree line, the sound of wood dragging against the cordura echoing out behind him.

The first shook his head as he debated following after. "Someone could get hurt!" he called. There was no response. As usual. He hesitated a moment. Then followed after.

The trees were easy to make out at least. The glow of the moon lent a cool, blue hue to everything around them. He found his companion waiting.

The two followed a dirt path that twisted around the silent pines, and crossed an old stone bridge before climbing up the hill that betrayed that this was the way home. Ahead the town lights painted the November clouds a rusty orange that stood out harshly in the night.

"Come on," the second boy urged from the crest of the hill.

The first lumbered up after him. He could see why his companion had stopped. The hill fell steeply into a depression littered with stones and broken bits of branches.

Now there were all sorts of things he thought about saying.

Can we actually climb down there? was the first thought.

Can we go around? was a close second.

But as the second boy pushed him over the edge he lost that train of thought. Surprise, surprisingly rushed in and took over. Not anger or even truly fear. Nothing but pure, unrestrained surprise. His thoughts scattered from there.

As his leg was caught, briefly between two stones, he considered calling for help. But as the force of his tumble broke the ankle, freeing his foot from its temporary hold that train departed as well.

When he finally came to a crashing stop in the center of the cluttered depression, he realized that there were in fact, no branches littered about and confirmed to himself that yes, he was just shoved down here.

"You pushed me," he said as he strained to sit up. The action highlighted the injury to his foot and pain forced him to lay still. "It's broken. I know it, it hurts. Why did you do that?" the first shouted through freshly welling tears.

"Why?" The second looked genuinely confused. That's when the first noticed they weren't alone. Beside his former companion, at waist height, a pair of amber eyes. And now that he could see them, they were everywhere.

Four, eight, sixteen, more.

"I told you," said the second. "It's time for dinner."

Imaginary Dreams
By Deana Burson

Childhood should be full of magical memories. At least, that was the mantra that we tried to live by. Preparing for the inevitable along with the doctors' uncertainty of time, made this difficult.

Watching her sleep was one of my greatest joys. That meant there was no pain, only dreams. I tried to imagine what her dreams consisted of. Dreams of Heaven? Dreams of ponies? Dreams of glittery pixie dust and Peter Pan? She would never tell me exactly what they were.

She would say, "Mom, I dream of your future. You are gonna love it there!"

Her excitement for my future shredded my heart each morning. I knew it was a future that wasn't going to include her. So I would smile, just like I did every morning, and dive in for a tickle fight. It kept her preoccupied while the nurses got ready for their morning "to do" list.

"Ok, sweetie," I said as the nurse began to hook up her IV drip. "It's time to get watered."

"Silly mom, I'm not a flower."

"You are my flower, sweetheart. You were planted in my heart."

Together we laid in her hospice bed, closed our eyes and planned our imaginary, action packed, fun-filled day.

The Crossing
By JoeTwo

Janis went to the stern where Bill, her cousin, had staked out a spot to watch the wake of the ship. He had talked about how the propellers of the ship made all of the little algae and creatures light up as they are churned so that you could see a trail of ghostly light. The sun had yet to set, but he was firmly placed content to wait.

"You don't see things like this every day Jan," he explained. "You should have more patience."

Patience was one thing Janis had in short supply. She had used up all she had left and it had ended up on the night boat. It was hard to believe that Bill could be taking this so stoically, especially considering that she had just told him that morning. Still he didn't quite act the same, hints that he was taking it harder than he let on. Acting coolly, for her sake.

Remembering all the times that her cousin had been there for her, Janis put her arm around Bill's neck. He held her hand tenderly.

"It's going to be alright Jan. We'll be there and back before anyone knows."

"I know!" Janis said back. "I'm just a little nervous."

As if on cue a man burst out of the door behind them, threw his head over the edge of the stern and started to throw up. Janis looked away from that display and into her cousin's eyes. They sat there quietly as the man finished, and green-faced, staggered back in through the door.

When the door slammed shut, they both started to laugh uncontrollably. The tension between them evaporating in a series of giggles.

"He must have eaten one of those dodgy sandwiches from the canteen," said Bill, after he had caught his breath, leading to them both convulsing in laughter again.

Their eyes were still glistening with laughter tears when Bill said to Janis, "Jan, I'm glad you trusted me with this. I couldn't bear the thought of you going through this alone."

Janis looked out over the increasingly dark water. "I know Billy. But I have to do this. Thank you for understanding."

Bill grabbed Janis' shoulder and turned her back to face him. "You know Jan, I know some lads from the club, hard men. If you were just to give me that bastard's name…"

But Janis placed her hand over Bill's mouth. "I've told you already not to do anything like that. There will be enough hurt after this is done for you be adding to it." She then turned back to face the sea. "Besides what if they find out back home?"

Bill nodded, sadly, in agreement. "Still, you know what that fucker is worth now, don't you?" He then put his arm over Janis' shoulder. Instinctively, she moved in closer to Bill, her arms lightly touching her belly, and together they stood, looking over the boiling water beneath them.

Haunted Keys
By Ermisenda Alvarez

My fingers nudged the door open. It was the last door standing. The battered room creaked and groaned in agony beneath my heavy footing. Despite the commotion outside, I felt alone for a moment. The silence of the room obliterated my senses. I could only see what was before me. A withered piano stood. Unable to resist, I lunged towards it.

My fingertips hesitated a centimeter above the keys. The image of my wife burned my mind: her delicate hands, her musical talent. I wasn't sure if the piano would wheeze out the melodies she had taught me or collapse beneath my hands. I couldn't risk it collapsing; I needed to hold on to the piano, the memory of her. No fingers touched those battered keys and yet a sweet, melancholic tune flooded the barren room and my scorched mind. It was her playing, I could hear it. I closed my eyes for a moment— the door was suddenly kicked down.

"Soldier, let's keep moving."

Sex on the Beach
By Anne Schilde

The driftwood sculpture danced in the flickering light of the beach fire. Missy and Tyler sat cuddled underneath the cavorting images set against the white glow of the firelight illuminating the ocean mist. Annie sucked down the last of her Sex on the Beach as she watched the shadowy ritual, mesmerized under her blanket wrap as the sounds of Jeff's guitar floated out over the lilt of the tumbling tide.

"What are you staring at, Pockets?" Billy asked.

Annie hesitated before answering, "At first I thought it was two stags battling, but now it looks like a bird attacking a giant scorpion."

Billy snorted. "No more drugs for you."

Annie made a face. "I'm not the one who doses myself on Morphine at the doctor's office."

Billy had in fact done just that, on top of a whole pretense that he needed brain surgery. He pretended he didn't hear Annie's comment.

"I think it looks like a boy and girl sucking face in public all rude like," Jessi offered.

Annie laughed. "Not Missy and Tyler, I meant our driftwood sculpture."

Missy and Tyler barely looked up from their kissing, not long enough to catch the look Jessi shot them.

"No, I know," she said. "I was actually serious. I think it looks like a man and a woman having sex, you know, and she's on top."

Annie's face wrinkled up. She reached under her blanket and into a pocket on the side of her pants. "I think you just have sex on the brain," she said, pulling out a bottle of nail polish.

Jessi turned to stare directly at Annie's face. "Maybe… and maybe I lied and I think it looks like two girls."

An uncomfortable lull in the conversation followed. The sounds Missy and Tyler were making in their impassioned slop fest grew prominent, making the thought impossible not to entertain. Just for a moment… the sounds of the ocean, the womb of all life, massaging their souls… It sent a little shudder through her body.

Billy interrupted the silence by playfully punching Annie in the shoulder. "Sex on the brain is better than drugs on the brain, Pockets. And you need another Sex on the Beach."

The punch pushed Annie's face closer to Jessi's and she looked into her best friend's eyes as the flickers of the flame danced across them. Their usual green turned to brown in the warm glow.

"What's up with you and the drugs, Billy?" she asked, still looking at Jessi. "You're the freak who's on drugs."

Billy was a freak. That was just a fact. And Billy was on drugs. Annie knew he and Jeff had burned before picking the rest of them up and she was pretty sure they'd sneaked off to re-up while they were all out hunting up driftwood for the sculpture. Jeff was so out there he might as well be on a different planet. He was completely lost in his guitar, strumming the same chords over and over in no recognizable songs. Billy refilled Annie's cup and set it in the sand next to her.

She unscrewed the cap of her polish and began to paint.

"Since when do you have nails?" Jessi asked, her attention suddenly called to the oddity of the polish. She grabbed Annie's hand for an inspection.

"You like?" Annie pulled her hand back before Jessi really had a chance to see.

"Who paints their fucking nails on the beach? That's what I want to know." Billy said.

Annie ignored him. She took a sip from her drink and went back to painting. "What do you think the driftwood looks like, Drughead?" she asked.

Billy stared out at their artistic erection. "Seriously? It looks like a bunch of fucking wood sticking out of the sand." When it didn't draw any laughs he added, "No Jessi's right. I can totally see the girl-on-girl thing. It's kind of hot."

Annie smiled. She screwed the cap back on her polish and drew another sip of her drink, scooting closer to the fire. She leaned forward and shoved her hands into the embers. Her freshly painted nails instantly erupted in flames and she pulled them out to admire them.

"Flower!" Jessi shrieked, slapping Annie's arm.

Missy and Tyler stopped kissing. Jeff stopped playing. For a tiny second the waves stopped crashing and even the driftwood stopped its entangled lovemaking.

"How hot is that?" Annie asked Billy, with a wild look in her eyes. She thrust her blazing digits into the cold sand to extinguish them. She wiggled them around a little. "I think I burned my fingertips off."

She pulled her hands up out of the sand. The fake nails were gone and her naked fingers were unharmed. "Since when do I have nails?" she grinned.

Jessi snatched up Annie's nail polish and smelled it. It reeked like pure acetone. "What the fuck is the matter with you, Flower?"

Annie shrugged. "I've been hanging around Billy too much, I guess."

Contortionist
By Nanda Fogli

I want no edges,
no verges,
no angles.

No tension,
spasms,
or throes.

I want to be elastic
and fit wherever
you let me go.

I'm a contortionist
trying to squeeze me
in your wild heart.

Chances
By Airicka Phoenix

Jacob wasn't a believer of things unanswerable. All things had answers; all things had a scientific explanation. But Angie had none of those things.

He could find no method to her madness, no sense to her constant ability to see things in Technicolor when life was a murky shade of gray. How could one person be so… carefree? Normal people weren't so happy! It was unnatural.

"Stop frowning, Jake." Her fingers were warm, prodding the corners of his mouth. Her laugh tinkled when he jerked back. "You're going to get wrinkles."

"I'm seventeen." He rubbed the tingling spot on his face. "I won't get wrinkles for another twenty years."

Again, she laughed, leaping to her feet and doing a twirl right there on the winding path cutting through the park. Her hair splayed out in the air, a glistening cape of shiny copper.

"Come on, Jake! Let's go do something fun!"

Fun? For him, that would be going home and looking over his biology paper. But with her, it could mean anything.

"Like what?"

Angie shrugged her dainty shoulder. "Let's go to the cliffs. It's almost sunset."

"There's a sixty percent chance it's going to rain—"

She rolled her pretty green eyes heavenwards, an

endearing smile tilting her lips. "You are always so serious! Besides, I think it would be romantic to be caught in the rain together."

Jacob couldn't help but wrinkle his nose. "What's so romantic about pneumonia?"

She shook her head, swooping down and grabbing his wrist. "Come on, Mr. Stick-In-The-Mud."

As affronted as he was by the name calling, he allowed himself to be yanked out of his seat and dragged to the other end of the park.

The cliffs overlooked a wide stretch of ocean, now churning with an impending storm. The sky in the distance was a murky gray, bleeding into red and orange. In his opinion, there was nothing remotely romantic about standing there with nothing but a painful death looming below them. However, Angie seemed pleased; she had a flush to her cheeks and a glow to her eyes that made them appear glassy. He would have been concerned if it wasn't an expression she wore often whenever they were together.

"Jake?" She turned those enormous eyes towards him. "Do you ever wish you could fly?"

Jacob thought about it as carefully as he would any other question before answering. "Well, that depends on what you mean. Do I wish I could sprout wings and take to the heavens? Then no, I don't."

There was a strange darkness in her eyes when she looked away, a flicker Jacob had never seen before. It was unlike her not to be glowing from the inside out.

"I always wish I could fly. I would go everywhere."

He started to tell her it was theoretically impossible; the world was too big for a single person to see everywhere in one lifetime. But something in the way she sighed kept him in check.

Then, just like that, she was smiling again, big and bright, eyes a little wild. "Hey, you know what we should do? We should jump!"

Maybe it was the glint behind her stare or the way her grip on his hand had tightened, but Jacob shuffled back a step. "What?"

"Come on! It'll be so much fun!"

"No!" He shook her hand off. "There are rocks at the bottom. The probability of us missing them..."

There was no smile on her face this time when she rolled her eyes. "Don't be such a baby! We'll aim away from the rocks."

"The winds are too strong!" Was he really standing there arguing this with her? "We're not jumping!"

"I am!" Then she was running, like a gazelle through the meadows.

For a moment, all he saw was floating hair, the billow of her skirt fluttering around her long legs. Her laughter caught the whistling wind and pounded in his ears. His heart jacked into his throat, stopping possibly all together if he could wrap his head around it. Every nerve in his body screamed as image after image flashed behind his eyes of her sailing over and disappearing from sight, from his life forever.

"No!" The scream tore his esophagus.

He couldn't recall lunging after her. He wasn't even sure when he'd moved. But he had her, a fistful of her dress in his grasp. Her yelp of surprise had never sounded so beautiful to him. He reeled her in like a fish on a hook, yanking her into the folds of his arms, crushing her.

"Are you crazy?" he growled into the top of her head. "Don't ever do that again!"

"I won't." There was a hint of a smile in her tone, but he didn't care when her arms found their way around him too.

Contributors

Alvarez, Ermisenda: Author of *Blind Sight Through the Eyes of Leocardo Reyes*, blogger at Ermilia

Ayers, Stephanie: blogger at My Write Side

Brindle, Kyllan: blogger at The Green Fox Press

Burson, Deana: blogger at My Thoughts on the Subject are as Follows

Coulthard, Melanie: blogger at The Poet's Hide

Fogli, Nanda: blogger at Cenicitas

Gemini: blogger at Simply Gemini

Hawthorne, Eliabeth: Author of *Blind Sight Through the Eyes of Aniela Dawson*, blogger at Ermilia

JoeTwo: blogger at Joe2Poetry

Judy, D.: blogger at An Evil Nymph's Blog

Lee-Anne: blogger at Oresh Memoirs

Lyon, Marisa: blogger at Marisa D. Lyon

Neal, AR: blogger at One Starving Activist

Nymus, Anna: blogger at Discoveries in a Letterbox

Otheus: Picture it & Write Contributor

Phoenix, Airicka: Author of *Touching Eternity*, blogger at Airicka Phoenix

Russell, Amber "Serene": Role player at Dae Luin

S., Devina: blogger at Hot Chocolate and Books

Schilde, Anne: blogger at Anne Schilde

Smith, Tanitha: blogger at The Mind of Tanitha

Tacken, Jenny: blogger at Ramblings from a Mum

Warren, Samantha: Author of *Vampire Assassin*, blogger at Samantha Warren - Author

Zshamaine, Karyl: blogger at The Eclectic Eccentric Shopaholic

Anonymous blogger at Korea, Love and Longing